In days of old the story's told,
of a knight both bold and brave.
He was strong and true,
{and humble too}
and his name was Fearless Dave.

For
Ami, Thomas, Elias, Caleb,
Matilda, Reuben, Alexander,
Babik, Lucien, Marius,
& Lola Mary - {The Sausage Fairy}

First published in Great Britain and the USA in 2006 by
Frances Lincoln Children's Books, 4 Torriano Mews,
Torriano Avenue, London NW5 2RZ
www.franceslincoln.com

Distributed in the USA by Publishers Group West

British Library Cataloguing in Publication Data available on request

ISBN 10: 1-84507-496-3
ISBN 13: 978-1-84507-496-8

Illustrated in ink and Photoshop

Printed in Singapore
1 3 5 7 9 8 6 4 2

FEARLESS DAVE
by
Bob Wilson
Being an historical account of a LEGENDARY BATTLE between an HEROIC KNIGHT and a HUGE HIDEOUS MONSTER
And the story of what *really* happened.

CASTLE TOURS
Queue here.
Next historic
tour 2 PM.

Castle Tours
YOUR GUIDE
Professor I Noah Lott (MA)

CASTLE TOURS
Queue here.

Long years ago a humble serf
Did in this township dwell.
How he became a valiant knight
Is the tale that I now tell.
CASTLE COMPUTERS
Young Dave was not of noble line.
Yet only he did heed,
The plaintive cries
of a fair princess,
In her hour of greatest need.

Back! Back! You hideous beast. Your fiendish claws don't frighten me.
For my heart is pure, my spirit bold...
...and my mighty blade both strong and...
Our David! Stop tormenting the poor cat and come here a minute.

What's up, Mum?
Look at this advert in the paper. Read what it says.
FOR SALE & WANTED
FOR SALE (Due to unexpected recovery) LARGE PINE COFFIN Would suit plague victim or similar
FOR SALE FOUR AND TWENTY DEAD BLACKBIRDS. IDEAL GIFT FOR SOMEONE WHO HAS A LARGE PIE-DISH
WANTED Person to help PRINCESS IN DISTRESS REWARD OFFERED Apply at Castle
WANTED For armed robbery. Mask, swag-bag and blunderbuss Must be in good condition
FOR SAL Large quar of PIG cheap
What d'you think?
I think I shall mount upon my trusty bicycle and ride to the castle at great speed.
I think I shall go with him in case he falls off.

Accompanied by his loyal page,
{A dame of three score years}
Young Dave did boldly venture forth
To calm a young maid's fears.

But ee'n before he'd rode a league,
Beyond the township's gate,
His bold endeavour was waylaid,
By the cruel, cold hand of fate.
Ye Olde Chip Shop

Oh, knickers!
What's up now?

I've got a puncture.
Well, leave your bike here. We'll walk.

But it's *miles.*
Don't be such a wimp...
...and take that bucket off your head. You look a right wally.

King Arfwitt and Queen Girdlestein
Were in the castle hall,
When Fearless Dave and his page arrived
In answer to their call.

Imagine how their hearts did leap,
How much they did rejoice
To see his rugged, manly frame,
To hear his noble voice.

Mornin', Your Royalships. Saw your advert. What's the problem.
The princess won't go into her bedroom.
She says there's a creature in there.
What sort of creature?
A horrid creature!

The creature Princess Peach had seen
Had given her such a scare,
She'd cried:-
"Eeek! Someone save me!"
And jumped on to a chair.
CLICK.
CLICK!
A CHAIR PROBABLY NOT ALL THAT DIFFERENT FROM THE ONE PRINCESS PEACH MIGHT HAVE JUMPED ON TO.
Young Dave did wait a while – and then,
When the young maid's tears had ceased,
He bade his goodly page enquire,
As to the nature of the beast.

Tell me, Princess. Did this creature let forth *a mighty roar*?
You know. Sort of like...
WHOAR!

No. It squeaked.
Squeaked?
It was a very *mighty* squeak.

This creature – was it by any chance breathing out ghastly plumes of *smoke and fire*?
You know. Sort of like...
Wooosh!

No. It was nibbling a lump of cheese.
Cheese?

I think it might have been *smoked* cheese.

What d'you think
it was, Mum?
A dragon.
A DRAGON!
Oh, how terribly awfully terrible.

I was hoping
she'd say that.

Hang on a tick.

I've never heard
of a dragon that
squeaks.
Nor one that
eats cheese.

What kind of dragon *squeaks?*
What kind of dragon eats cheese?
Err...
?
A Squeaky Cheese-Eating Dragon.
And they're the worst kind!

"Oh, woe! Oh, woe!"

wailed Princess Peach.

"Oh, lack-a-day!"

she cried.

"Be still, my sweet young maid. Be still."
Dave's goodly page did chide.

"Fear not," spake she. "Though mighty dread,
Hath seized your troubled mind.
Glad tidings do I bring to you,
To you, and all mankind."

Our David'll slay the dragon for you – no problem. He's a dab hand at that sort of thing.
Sorry. Not allowed.
Only knights are allowed to slay dragons.
Do you know the qualifications you need to have if you want to become a knight?
No. But I'd like to know. I bet they're more interesting than the qualifications you need to have if you want to become an assistant pig-swill strainer like what me dad was.
I was hoping he'd say that.

In days of yore it was the law
If one wished to become a knight,
One had to be fearless, brave, and bold.
{And preferably not too bright.}

So, tell me young man. Are you bold?

YES.
I like a man who's bold.

Are you as bold as Sir Ulgar the Unbeatable who boldly battled with the diabolical dragons of Denmark?
I'm not sure.
How bold was Sir Ulgar the Unbeatable who did boldly battle with the diabolical dragons of Denmark?

Sir Ulgar the Unbeatable was uncommonly bold, 'tis said.

His body lies inside this tomb...

...they never found his head.

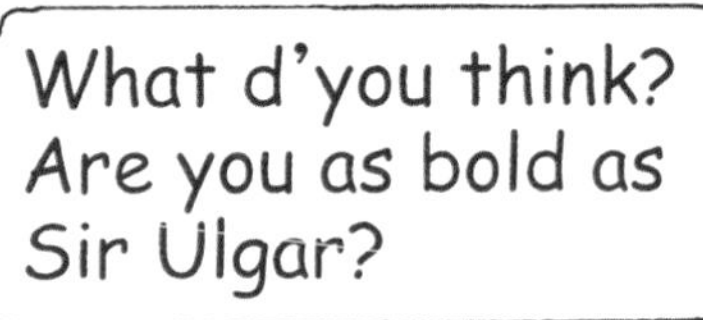
What d'you think? Are you as bold as Sir Ulgar?

?

No.

Excuse me, your Majesty. I'd just like to point out in case you hadn't noticed. He may not be as bold as Sir Ulgar but...

...he's still got
his own head.

You can't kiss a man
if he's got no head.
She's not wrong.

A knight has to be
brave as well as bold.
Are you brave?
Oh, yes.
At least I
think I am.
I like a man who
thinks before he
speaks.
Depends how
brave you mean.

Are you as brave as Sir Duncan McDaft who deliberately defied danger, and whose daring deeds deserve to be dramatically described and dynamically depicted in song, verse and possibly a village maypole dance?
Err...
I don't know.

What daring deed did he do?

When Sir Duncan McDaft fought the dragons of Doom, He was really, really brave.
We know that this be true because...

...it says so on his grave.
HERE
LIES THE BODY OF
SIR DUNCAN MCDAFT
Not all of his body obviously. Once the dragons had stomped on him a few times there wasn't much left for us to bury that wasn't already 6ft underground. But we did find a bit of his left ear-lobe and one of his fingers. Least we think it was a finger. It could have been a dead worm – or anything really.
Can you imagine yourself doing what Sir Duncan did?
Err?
No.
Listen, Your Majesty. He may have no imagination and he might not be very brave – but I'll tell you what...

He's got a full set of body parts.

You can't cuddle a man if he's got no body.
Women know about these things.

Besides being uncommonly bold and really, really brave a knight has to be fearless. Tell me young man, are you afraid of anything?
?
Men who say there's nothing they're afraid of are usually either lying or boasting.
Yes. Actually, there is one thing I'm afraid of ...
I'll tell you what it is!

He's afraid that if he tells you that there's nothing he's afraid of you'll think he's either lying or boasting.

And anyway, you've not got time for all that who's-afraid-of-what business now...
Your daughter wants a word.

Tho' days be dark, true love, like fruit,
Still ripens on the bough.
And so it was with Princess Peach
That love did bloom, and now...
Inside the breast of that fair maid
Was kindled such a fire,
She threw all caution to the wind
And spoke her heart's desire.

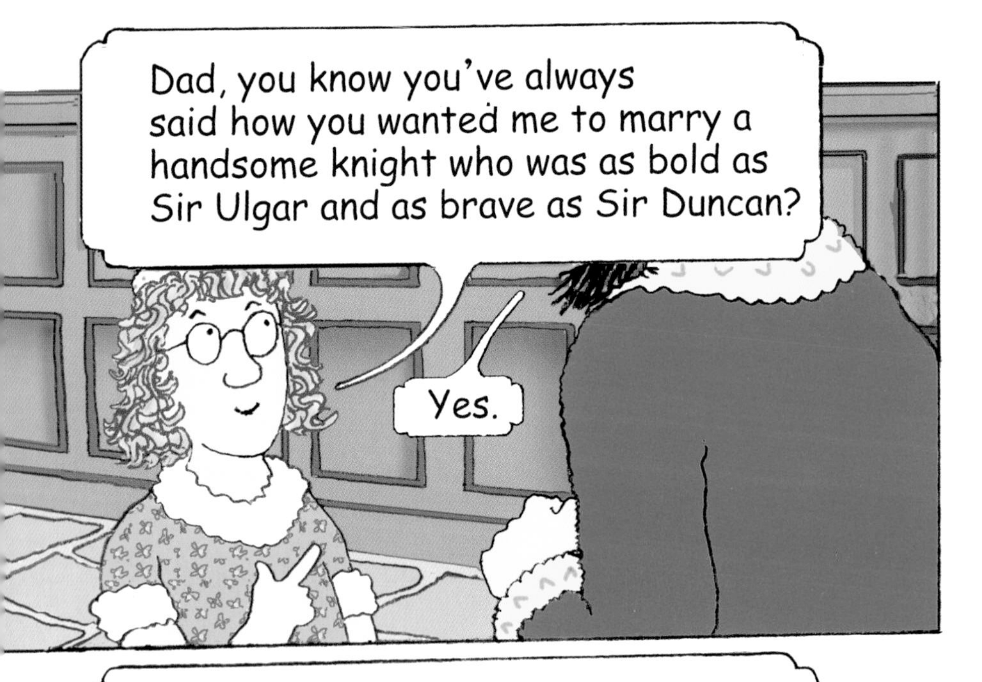
Dad, you know you've always said how you wanted me to marry a handsome knight who was as bold as Sir Ulgar and as brave as Sir Duncan?
Yes.

Well, to be honest, I think I'd rather marry a fairly bold, moderately brave knight who's still got a head and a full set of working body parts.
I was hoping she'd say that.

Though mindful of the terrible risks,
Entwined in such a task
As slaying an awesome dragon,
Dave's page did straightways ask
If Dave did slay the fiendish beast,
Would the king make him a knight
And let him marry Princess Peach?
To which the King replied ...

...All right.
Just so long as he doesn't get blood and body parts all over the carpet.

We've only just had it cleaned from the last time.
Fair enough.

"My Liege, 'tis time!"
{The page proclaimed},
"For thee to show thy worth.
So don thine armour, gird thy loins,
For we must sally forth."

In other words – put your bucket on, sunshine. It's time for us to go a-dragon slaughtering.
Oh, right.

Mum, you know how you told the King that I wasn't afraid of anything?
Yes.
Well, that's not exactly true because...
Shh! We haven't got time for that now.
Here's the door. Get ready. *We're going in.*

What horrors lay behind that door,
None but the Princess knew.
T'was for the sake of that fair maid,
That Dave went boldly through.

Imagine then how she did feel,
How terrified and tense,
When an awful scream did rent the air
As a battle did commence.

EeeeeeK!
Here we go. Fight's started.
Oh, dear. I'm really terrified and tense...
...and hopeful, of course!

Help!
Someone save me!
Whack!
Whack!
Whack!
PP

Our David! Stop waving that sword about. You're going to end up doing yourself a mischief...

...and get down off that chair before you fall off.
But I saw a mouse, Mum. And I'm afraid of mice.

I know that, son. But it's gone now. I've caught it and put it back down the hole where it came from.
Oh, that's all right then.

Let's go get that dragon.
What dragon?
The Princess said she'd seen a dragon.
No, she didn't. *I* did.

You mean there *is* no dragon?
That's right.
I don't get it.
You will.

Then all was silent and t'was feared,
That Fearless Dave was dead.
But lo! His goodly page appeared,
Stood boldly forth, and said...

Fight's over. The dragon lost. Technical knockout in the first round.

The King and Queen were verily pleased.
To hear this proclamation.
And Princess Peach
(Who'd feared Dave dead)
Was filled with admiration.

Now, about the wedding. Have you thought about where we're going to have the reception?

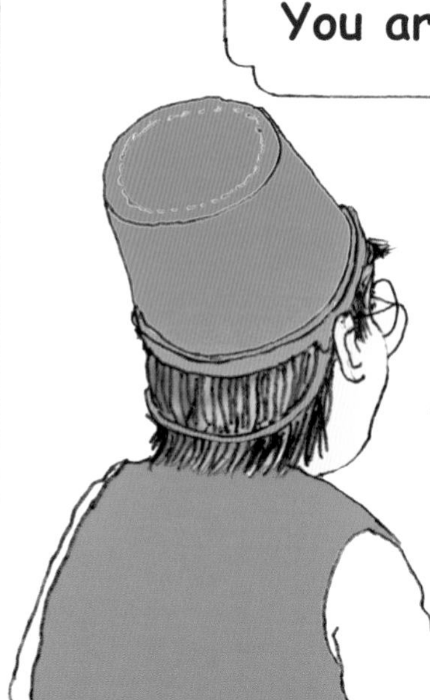

Oh, Dave. You saved me from the terrible Squeaky Cheese-Eating Dragon **You are *such* a hero.**
Well, not really. You see ...

It wasn't a dragon. It was...
Ssh! I know what it was *really*. Don't worry. I'll marry you anyway.
I was hoping she'd say that.

Of such events is history made,
And this the King knew well.
So he bid his learned scribe record,
That which there was to tell.

First of all, tell me. Was it a big creature?
No. I wouldn't say it was big. I'd say it was...

...ABSOLUTELY HUGE!
But our Dave didn't give a monkey's how big it was. He just...
The creature was of awesome girth, But Sir Dave was not bowed down
...whacked it on the bonce good and hard **Whack! Whack! Whack!**
Three times he struck a mighty blow, 'Pon the evil monster's crown

Then the thing went absolutely doolally and charged at our Dave but he dodged and tripped it over, and before it could get up again he gave it a right good kick up the bum, and the thing went – ***'Arrrgh!'*** No. Sorry. I meant – ***'Squeak! Squeeak!'*** – and ran off like a bat out of hell.
The beast then made a fearsome lunge.
But our brave resourceful knight,
Was favoured by good fortune's smile,
For the end was now in sight.
With one tremendous, well-aimed blow,
He smote the beast – and then
It roared in anguish, turned and fled,
And ne'er was seen again

And here it is – the very book
In which the scribe did write.
It tells how a hideous dragon
Was slain by a bold, brave knight.
It tells how a princess got her wish:
A husband, bold and brave,
Who was strong and true, and humble too,
And whose name was FEARLESS DAVE.

And they both lived happily
ever after.
THE END
Actually, it's
not quite the end.

David, dearest. I've been thinking. Seeing as you're now a prince I don't think it's right that your mother should have to carry on living in that flea-ridden, rat-infested hovel down in the village. I think she should come up to the castle and live with us where she can wallow in unbridled luxury and be waited on hand and foot.

THE END